First edition

Published by Ladybird Books Ltd Loughborough Leicestershire UK

Printed in England (7)

Disney

Peter Pan

Ladybird Books

Every night at bedtime, Wendy Darling told her brothers John and Michael wonderful stories about a faraway place called Never Never Land, where a boy called Peter Pan lived.

One night something amazing happened. Peter Pan himself came to take the children on a magical journey. Peter's friend Tinker Bell the fairy sprinkled the children with pixie dust, and soon they were all flying – out of the window, up into the sky, and away to Never Never Land!

When they got to Never
Never Land, Peter told
Tinker Bell to introduce
the children to his friends
the Lost Boys.

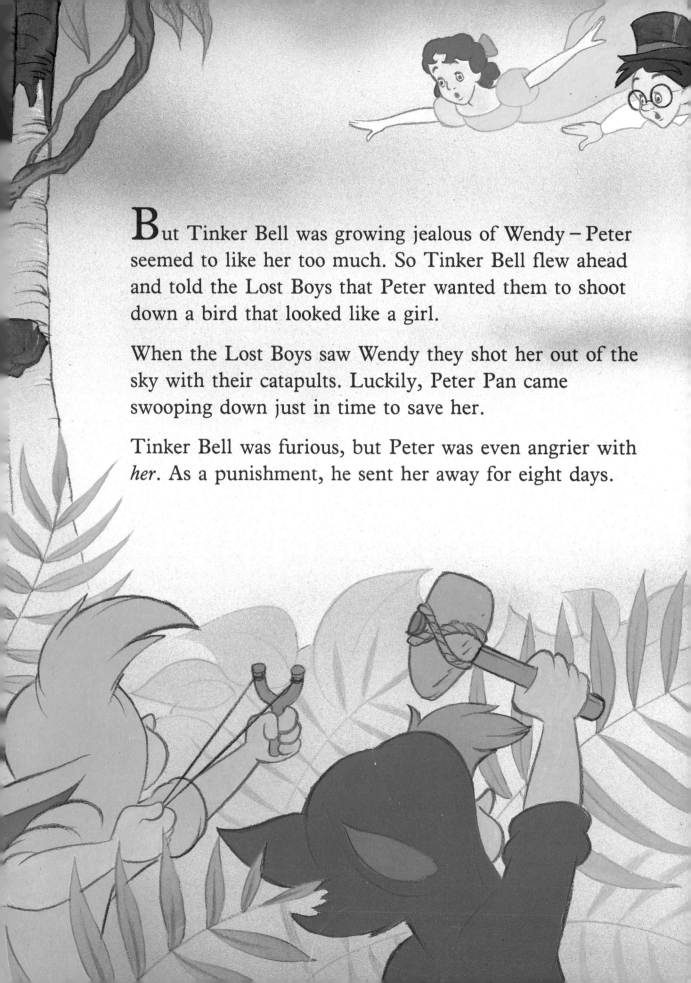

But Tinker Bell was growing jealous of Wendy – Peter seemed to like her too much. So Tinker Bell flew ahead and told the Lost Boys that Peter wanted them to shoot down a bird that looked like a girl.

When the Lost Boys saw Wendy they shot her out of the sky with their catapults. Luckily, Peter Pan came swooping down just in time to save her.

Tinker Bell was furious, but Peter was even angrier with *her*. As a punishment, he sent her away for eight days.

Peter took Wendy off to do some sightseeing, and left John in charge of Michael and the Lost Boys. Happily, John led them all through the forest in search of adventure.

And what an adventure they had! The boys hadn't gone far when they were captured by a band of Indian braves.

"We're holding you all prisoner until we find out who's kidnapped our Chief's daughter, Princess Tiger Lily," the Indians said.

At that very moment, Peter Pan and Wendy were peering down from a high ledge overlooking the sea. An evil-looking pirate had just tied up Princess Tiger Lily and left her on a rock.

"That's Captain Hook!" Peter whispered to Wendy. "He's been my enemy for as long as I can remember. And Tiger Lily is my friend!"

Captain Hook's menacing voice echoed through the lagoon. "Tell me where Peter Pan's hiding place is," he ordered Tiger Lily, "or I'll leave you here to drown when the tide comes in."

Tiger Lily was frightened, but she said bravely, "I'll never tell you. Never!"

Peter didn't wait another second. He flew down and challenged Captain Hook.

Up and down the rocky cliffs they fought, until Captain Hook lost his footing and fell into the sea.

As Hook's boatman, Mr Smee, rescued the captain, Peter untied Tiger Lily. "Beat you again, Hook!" he called, as he flew off with the princess safely in his arms.

The Big Chief was so grateful to see his daughter safe and sound that he made Peter Deputy Big Chief. Then he set all the boys free and threw a big party, complete with feasting, singing and dancing.

After the peace pipe was passed round, Wendy and the boys went back to Peter's secret cave to rest after their adventures.

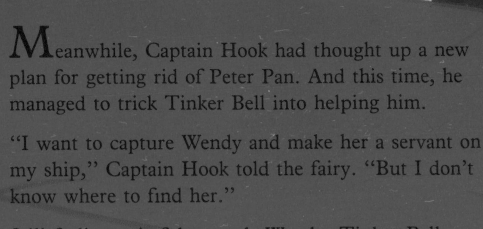

Meanwhile, Captain Hook had thought up a new plan for getting rid of Peter Pan. And this time, he managed to trick Tinker Bell into helping him.

"I want to capture Wendy and make her a servant on my ship," Captain Hook told the fairy. "But I don't know where to find her."

Still feeling spiteful towards Wendy, Tinker Bell was only too pleased to help Captain Hook. She dipped her toes in a bottle of ink and danced lightly across a map of Never Never Land. Her footprints showed the way to Peter's cave.

That was all Captain Hook needed. Chuckling wickedly, he locked Tinker Bell in a glass cage and set off to carry out his evil plan.

ack at the cave, the children were all getting homesick. They decided it was time to return to their mothers and fathers again.

The Lost Boys left first. Then Michael and John said goodbye to Peter Pan. Wendy was the last to go. "I'll never forget you, Peter," she said.

By now the pirates were lying in wait just outside the cave. As the children came out, they grabbed them, one by one. They gagged the children, tied them up, and took them back to their ship.

As soon as the children were gone, Captain Hook left a parcel outside Peter's door, with a label that said: *To Peter from Wendy*. "This should finish him off," the Captain said, grinning.

But Tinker Bell had seen Captain Hook wrapping the parcel, and she knew what was in it – a bomb! Using all her strength, she broke out of her glass cage and flew off to warn Peter Pan.

Aboard the pirate ship, the children had been tied to a mast. "We'll give you a choice," snarled the pirates. "Either join our pirate band, or walk the plank and drown!"

The boys quite liked the idea of
being pirates, but Wendy refused to
betray Peter. Bravely, she started
down the plank. Everyone waited
for the splash as she stepped off
the end.

But the splash never came. Tinker
Bell had reached Peter Pan in time
to warn him about the bomb and to
tell him where the children were.
He arrived just in time to catch
Wendy as she fell.

"Hurrah for Peter Pan!" cheered the boys. But Captain Hook was seething with rage.

"I'll get you this time, Peter Pan!" he screamed as he drew his sword.

Quick as a flash, Peter drew his dagger, and the two began a breathtaking duel.